D1404959

THE STORY OF OLAF

THE STORY OF

olaf

By JAMES & RUTH McCREA

Atheneum / New York / 1964

J
McCrae

FOR AUNT LOUISE

Once upon a time, in an old castle,

there lived two brave knights,

Sir Charles and Sir Egbert, and

Sir Charles
and Sir Egbert
had fine days
riding their horses
and being brave,
while Olaf chased
hummingbirds
with his little red flag.
Although their castle
was neither big nor
grand, they were
very happy—except
for one thing.

Olaf, the page boy.

Not far from the castle, in the middle
of a dark forest, lived a fierce dragon. He
trampled the flowers, frightened the children,
and spread terror throughout the land.
At night he roared so loudly that the children
cried, and the grownups could not sleep.

One morning, after a particularly roary night, Sir Charles grumbled to Sir Egbert. "This has to stop! Aren't we the bravest knights for miles around?"

"Yes indeed," said Sir Egbert. "We are the only knights in the whole countryside."

"So," said Sir Charles, "it is very clear. There is a knightly duty to be done. We must get rid of that dragon!"

"Oh my!" said Sir Egbert.

"Oh dear!" said Olaf.

Sir Charles went to the window and scowled out at the forest. He was thinking.

"I know how to do it," he said. "But first we must see old Erfurt, the wizard."

Olaf saddled the horses. When all was
ready, he climbed up behind Sir Egbert,
and off they rode to see Erfurt.

"Change us into dragons!" said the knights.

Erfurt looked at them in surprise.

"Why dragons?" he asked.

"To catch one, of course," said Sir Charles.
"Everyone knows it takes a dragon to
catch a dragon." What a booby!
he thought to himself, for all
his being a wizard.

Old Erfurt shook his head.
"I can change you into
dragons easily enough,
but I am not sure that
that is the best way—"

But the two knights insisted. So Erfurt opened his monstrous big cupboard where he kept his wizard supplies and began rummaging inside. At last he held up a small bottle.

"Here is a magic potion," he said. "One teaspoon at bedtime, and in the morning you will be dragons."

The three thanked him kindly.
As they were leaving, Erfurt
whispered something
in Olaf's ear.

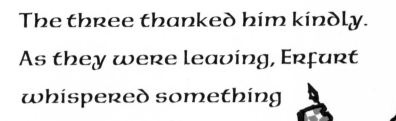

Olaf smiled back and waved
good-bye with his little red flag.
Then, holding the potion bottle very
carefully, the three rode back to the castle.

That night,
after Olaf was asleep,
Sir Charles
measured the potion
—one teaspoon
—it was very bitter.
Then,
leaving Olaf behind,
the two knights
rode off to the forest.

All night they waited. In the morning they were
dragons! They knew what they had to do.

They found the dragon in his cave, and,

after a dreadful battle, he fell down

—quite dead!

But alas!
Now there were
two dragons
instead of one,
and two less knights
than there were
before!

Poor Olaf!

When he awoke,

he was all alone.

He knew what had happened,

but he didn't know what to do.

Then he saw the potion bottle
where Sir Charles had left it.
He picked it up. There was still
some left in the bottom.
If I drink it, he thought,
I too will become a dragon!
But that would only make
another dragon—. Suddenly
he remembered Erfurt's words.

I MUST FACE THE DRAGONS AS A MAN!

He tucked the bottle
in his pocket
and set out for the forest.
He tried to be brave.

He looked on one side of the forest,
and he looked on the other side of the forest.

He looked at the top of the hill,
and he looked at the
bottom of the hill.

At last, in the mouth of a dark cave,
he found them. They were sleeping.
Olaf wanted to run away, but he didn't.
Instead, he crept nearer . . .
and nearer . . . and
nearer . . .

When he was quite close, he took the bottle
from his pocket and sprinkled a few drops
on each of the dragons.

Then he ran!

When he reached the edge of the forest,
he was so tired he could not run any farther.
He fell down on the grass, and soon
he was fast asleep.

Some time later, after the potion drops had
done their magic, Sir Charles and Sir Egbert
came out of the forest, knights once again.
They saw Olaf asleep in the grass. They
picked him up and, being very careful not to
wake him, carried him back to the castle.

The news spread quickly that the dragon had been killed. When the King heard of Olaf's part

in the affair, he proclaimed a great celebration
in order that such bravery could be rewarded.

Now in the forest there are no more dragons,
and in the castle live three brave knights:
Sir Charles, Sir Egbert, and

Sir Olaf!

Sir Charles
and Sir Egbert
have fine days
riding their horses
and being brave,
while Sir Olaf
chases hummingbirds
with his little red flag.

Although their castle
is neither big nor grand,
they are very happy.

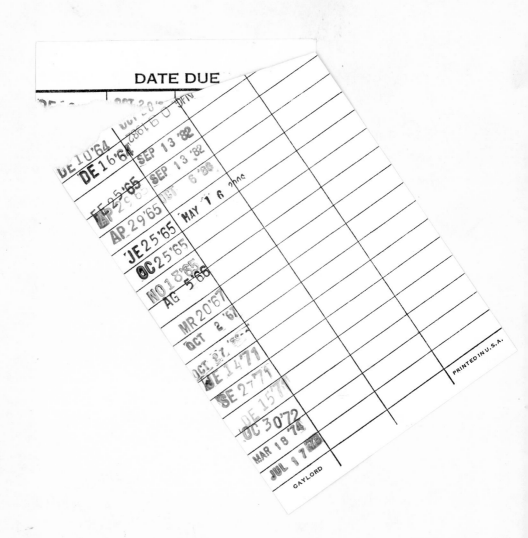

DATE DUE

DE 10'64	OCT 20'75	
DE 16'64	SEP 13 '82	
FE 25'65	SEP 13 '82	
AP 29'65	OCT 6 '86	
AP 29'65	MAY 1 6 2008	
JE 25'65		
OC 25'65		
NO 18'65		
AG 5'66		
MR 20'67		
OCT 2'67		
OCT 27'69		
SE 14'71		
SE 27'71		
SE 15'71		
OC 30'72		
MAR 18 74		
JUL 1 7 2008		